THE METAPHYSICS OF KNOWLEDGE

MAXWELL PRESS

THE METAPHYSICS OF KNOWLEDGE

ROGER B. C. JOHNSON

Professor of Philosophy in Miami University

Edited by

ALEXANDER T ORMOND

McCosh Professor of Philosophy

MAXWELL PRESS

Chennai   New Delhi

MAXWELL PRESS

An Imprint of MJP Publishers

ISBN 978-93-5528-203-3   MAXWELL PRESS

No. 44, Nallathambi Street,
Triplicane,
Chennai 600 005

MJP 1406   © Publishers, 2022

Publisher :   **C. Janarthanan**

PUBLISHER'S NOTE

The legacy of a country is in its varied cultural heritage, historical literature, developments in the field of economy and science. The top nations in the world are competing in the field of science, economy and literature. This vast legacy has to be conserved and documented so that it can be bestowed to the future generation. The knowledge of this legacy is slowly getting perished in the present generation due to lack of documentation.

Keeping this in mind, the concern with retrospective acquiring of rare books has been accented recently by the burgeoning reprint industry. MAXWELL PRESS is gratified to retrieve the rare collections with a view to bring back those books that were landmarks in their time.

In this effort, a series of rare books would be republished under the banner, "MAXWELL PRESS". The books in the reprint series have been carefully selected for their contemporary usefulness as well as their historical importance within the intellectual. We reconstruct the book with slight enhancements made for better presentation, without affecting the contents of the original edition.

Most of the works selected for republishing covers a huge range of subjects, from history to anthropology. We believe this reprint edition will be a service to the numerous researchers and practitioners active in this fascinating field. We allow readers to experience the wonder of peering into a scholarly work of the highest order and seminal significance.

MAXWELL PRESS

PREFACE.

It is now generally conceded that one of the most important contributions to English ethics during the last twenty-five years is Green's Prolegomena to Ethics. Its importance is due to two facts: (1) the systematic thoroughness with which, what, at the time of its appearance, was for the philosophic Briton a somewhat peculiar and foreign mode of thinking was made to do service in giving a reasoned foundation for ethical speculation; and (2) to the spirit of moral earnestness which its pages have caught from the personality of its author. My discussion will ignore the man and deal with his thought. I propose to examine some phases of Green's *theory of reality* as this is found in the first hundred pages or so of the Prolegomena, using other parts of his philosophical writings as they happen to throw light on these pages, which contain the essence of his constructive thinking. We find here, articulated in logical form and sequence, the basal ideas underlying all the penetrating and exhaustive criticism to which Green subjected the various forms of the national empiricism. This criticism has been called "victorious" by one of the most notable of Green's critics. What, then, are the data and the method of the rival metaphysical system? What is its own theory of the Real? What, for it, does experience and the analysis of experience mean? How does it reach truth and expose to view the fundamental conditions of knowledge and so of the Real? These are questions which I propose to examine briefly in the light of Green's answers.

Among recent writers whose works have been of special assistance to me in the prosecution of my philosophical studies, I wish to mention Professor Royce and Mr. F. H. Bradley. I am also under obligation to my friend, Professor A. T. Ormond of Princeton University, for instruction received from the penetrating discussion of fundamental philosophical notions to be found in his " Basal Concepts of Philosophy," and also for suggestions and friendly encouragement in my work. My first interest in ethics and metaphysics was awakened by the stimulating teaching of President Francis L. Patton; and it was he who first interested me in the philosophy of Green. My many other obligations can partly be seen by consulting the bibliography to be found at the close of this paper.

METAPHYSICS OF KNOWLEDGE.

I.

During the last twenty-five years, no attempt among English speaking people to offer a reasoned and systematic account of the nature of ultimate reality has been productive of more fruitful criticism and suggestion than that of Green. No other single force has been so effective in the exposure of the fundamental inconsistencies and contradictions of the national empiricism, inherited through a long line of ancestors from Locke and Hume. Whatever may be said of the success or failure of Green's own constructive conception of the Real considered as a system, it may be conceded, without fear, that his polemical work represents the high-water mark of English philosophical criticism. But to those acquainted with his philosophical activity as a whole, it is well known that this criticism moves throughout under the lead of a certain idealistic interpretation of the nature of the Real. His "central conception is that the universe is a single activity or energy, of which it is the essence to be self-conscious, that is, to be itself and not itself in one. Of this activity . . . every particular existence is a limited manifestation, and among other such existences, those which we call ' ourselves.' In so far as there is a ' we ' at all and a world which may be called ' ours,' it is because the self which is the unity of the world is communicated under the particular conditions of our physical organization. . . . The conception of self-consciousness as the ultimate reality is one to which we are led by reflecting upon our experience, or, in other words, by asking what we mean by a fact. It makes no difference whether fact be taken in the minimum or maximum of its meaning, whether, as the simplest possible fact, expressible as merely 'something,' or as the highly complex facts, covered by such words as 'science,' 'art,' 'morality,' or as the all-inclusive fact which we call 'the world.' At whatever point it is considered, it is found to consist in relationship or relationships. That which is simply itself is nothing; the reality of everything lies in its pointing beyond itself to something else; in other words, the real is something which is itself and not itself in one, a unity in difference or differentiated unity. If for instance reality be considered where it is at its least, where it can be indicated merely as 'this,' the fact so indicated can only be fully expressed as 'this not that,' in which each constituent is nothing without the other and the two together make a unity which is both and neither of them. . . . Lastly, if we ask ourselves what we mean by complete reality, the world or universe, the answer must be, 'a system in which every element, being correlative to every other, at once presupposes and is presupposed by every other,' a unity which distinguishes itself from and finds itself in, not this or that thing, but everything. All fact, then, or matter of expericnee, consists in relationship, and relationship implies self-consciousness, the only thing that we know 'in which a manifold is united without ceasing to be a manifold.'" [1]

This conception, expounded in systematic form in the opening chapters of the Prolegomena, and recurring in one form or another throughout the rest of his philosophical works, is made to do special service in the formation of a foundation for his doctrine of morality. Indeed, it is in connexion with his ethical interests that he is directly led to a systematic exposition and defense of those relatively fragmentary insights which had constituted the informing and quickening spirit of his criticism. The conception of

---

[1] Works of T. H. Green, Vol. III, pp. LXXV—LXXVI. An eXcellent summary may also be found in Mind, Vol. IX, pp. 75-76—in Balfour's article on Green's Metaphysics of Knowledge. Cf. also Mind, Vol. VIII. E. Caird on "Professor Green's Last Work."

ultimate reality as self-consciousness, as spirit, is necessary, according to this mode of thinking, if there is to be any such distinctive thing as a moral life at all. For just as self-consciousness is the principle, and the sole principle in terms of which our experience becomes an intelligible unity or cosmos; just as without it the world of nature becomes a world without meaning; so it is the principle without which the moral life is denuded of. all that makes it distinctively what it is. This principle, then, is the necessary foundation of ".ethics as a system of precepts."[2] The exhaustive discussion of this point (*i. e.*, the nature of reality as ultimately spiritual) has had as its purpose, he says,[3] the establishment of " some conclusion in regard to the relation between man and nature, a conclusion which must be arrived at before we can be sure that any theory of ethics, in the distinctive sense of the term, is other than wasted labor;" and the result of this discussion shows that an analysis of the facts of experience, which takes cognizance of them, not as abstractions, but in their concrete reality, implies in order to their intelligibility and existence as facts, the existence of a self-distinguishing consciousness. To give rational defense to this doctrine is the work of metaphysics, which is " the progressive effort towards a fully articulated conception of the world as a rational."[4] This defense seems necessary to Green (in spite of the apparent remoteness of metaphysics from that life with which morality seems to be directly concerned) because of the influence of the traditional empiricism in reducing man to a " being who is simply a result of natural forces " — a reduction which in strict thinking rendered the theoretical side of ethics nothing else than a discussion of laws belonging to a natural science and abolished "the practical or preceptive part altogether."[5] For if man be

---

[2] Cf. Seth's Hegelianism and Personality, p. 4.

[3] Prolegomena to Ethics, p. 54, section 52.

[4] Green's Works, Vol. III, p. LXXI ; cf. also Bradley's Appearance and Reality, p. 1.

[5] Fairbrother, The Philosophy of T. H. Green, p. 10 ; Prolegomena, etc., p. 9.

merely a natural being, conduct becomes describable in terms of natural fact, and it is absurd to say of a natural fact, or of a series of natural facts that it either ought or ought not to be.[6]

Bentham's phrase becomes pathetically appropriate—"if the use of the word (ought) be admissible at all, it 'ought' to be banished from the vocabulary of morals." This state of things may be characterized by saying that a large body of the English public persisted in the use of words, the meaning of which the current national philosophy had rendered nugatory. But what can be more unsatisfactory than this breach between life and thought—between thinking that a thing is true and then belying the thought by acting as if it were a falsehood? Let us then ask for the origin of this contradiction and let us get our answer through a critical analysis of both nature and man. For it is useless to discuss the question of a natural science of conduct until we have antecedently determined what we mean by nature. If 'nature' turn out to mean a 'connexion of matters of fact,' it then becomes necessary to ask how in experience such a connexion of matters of fact is possible. The possibility of this connexion may throw light on the relation of man to nature; may show that the self-conscious being whose self-consciousness is the necessary condition of there being such a thing as nature at all, is not himself a product of nature;[7] may show that "the subject of the categories" as Kant says,[8] "cannot, therefore, for the very reason that it cogitates these, frame any conception of itself as an object of the categories; for to cogitate these, it must lay at the foundation its own pure self-consciousness—the very thing that it wishes to explain and describe."

Driven out of the individualistic form in which it was

---

[6] Prolegomena, etc., p. 9, Sec. 7.

[7] Cf. Fairbrother, loc. cit., pp. 12, 13—for an account of Green's use of the term 'nature.' See also Green, Prolegomena, etc., p. 47, section 45 and pp. 56, 57, 58.

[8] Kant's Critique of Pure Reason (Meiklejohn) p. 249.

held by Hume and the Mills, the naturalistic account of man's relation to nature, next appears in the evolution doctrine of Spencer. But important as the doctrine of evolution unquestionably is in science (including psychology and sociology), it is very easy to over-emphasize its importance to metaphysics. The evolutionary doctrine of Spencer, which seems so superior to the individualistic empiricism of Hume, really gives the go-by to the genuinely metaphysical questions. It really assumes 'the order of nature' and then, by making use of the principle of hereditary transmission, it imagines that it has accounted for those "ideas of relation which seem to determine, not to result from, the experience of the individual."[9] The real question, however, is thus only pushed further back, to-wit—'How is such an order of nature possible?' Thus the evolution doctrine of Spencer, which never really touches "the real point of the controversy about *a priori* ideas, is commonly regarded as its final settlement."[10] Again, "given a world of intelligible relations, it is easy to account for knowledge. The modern 'experientialist' is taking the reality of such a world for granted along with a theory of reality which excludes it. Hume was trying to explain it away in order that the same theory of reality — the theory which identifies it with feeling—might be consistently maintained."[11] It thus becomes necessary, in view of the unintelligibility to which this empirical theory reduces our knowledge of man and the world, to state the problem in some such form as that in which it is found in Kant, viz., 'How is knowledge possible'? This question must not, however, be interpreted as "inviting any one to inquire whether he can do that which he constantly is doing, and must do in the very act of ascertaining whether he can do it. . . . It is simply the consideration of what is implied in the fact of our

<hr>

[9] Green's Works, Vol. I, p. 382 ; see also Bradley, App. and Reality, p. 137.

[10] Green's Works, Vol. I, p. 382.

[11] Green's Works, Vol. I, p. 382 ; see also Royce's Conception of God, p. 352.

knowing or coming to know a world, or conversely, in the fact of there being a world for us to know." [12] What is Green's answer to this question? What is his doctrine of the Real?

The Idealism, which is our heritage from Kant and his successors, enables us now to state the problem of philosophy in terms which, while verbally agreeing with pre-Kantian thought, have become charged with new meaning. Philosophy is still the theory of the Real and its method is still the analysis of experience, but the great movement of thought which Kant inaugurated and which may be said to have culminated in Hegel, has taught us the necessity of being very serious with this word 'experience.' [13] That. experience is the true point of departure of all philosophies is, I suppose, at the present time a universal belief. The resolution of experience into its last elements of analysis and the interpretation of the relationship between these may, indeed, be called the true problem of philosophy. But then, see the vast differences of opinion which emerge in interpreting the analytical result of the study of this same experience! [14] See the vast difference between the analysis of Locke and that of Kant! Every sane philosophy does appeal in the last result to experience, but the satisfactoriness of the philosophy depends finally upon what it understands as the. meaning of the concept 'experience.' For example, Green's whole transcendental theory is an elaborate and reasoned protest against the analysis of experience reached through the empiricism of Hume and his English followers. As Hegel says (p. 81 Logic. Wallace's translation.) " In what we call Experience there are two elements. The one

---

[12] Green's Works, Vol. I, p. 374 ; cf. also Watson's Kant and His English Critics, pp. 3, 4, 5, etc.

[13] Cf. Royce's Conception of God, p. 32.

[14] Cf. Prolegomena, etc., p. 19 (bottom of page). Here Green is exposing to view the fundamentally different ideas which underlie two of the interpretations of the concept of 'experience'-—the difference between 'change' and 'consciousness of change.'

is the matter, infinite in its multiplicity, and as it stands, a mere set of singulars: ' the other is the form, the characteristics of universality and necessity. Hume assumes the truth of the empirical element, feeling and sensation, and proceeds to challenge universal principles and laws, because they have no warranty from sense perception," (p. 82.) "It must be noted that the single sensation is not the same as experience, and that the Empirical school elevates the facts included under sensation, feeling, perception into the form of general ideas, propositions or laws. This, however, it does with the reservation that these general principles (such as force) are to have no further import or validity of their own beyond that taken from the sense impression . . . " [15]

Against such a reduction of experience to its last elements in mere sense-impressions, Green claims, with Hegel, that such a theory would, if it were consistent, be speechless. The attempt to build up the world of our supposed knowledge on the data of mere sense, either results in plunging us into a scepticism which cannot even rationally *call* itself scepticism or in the smuggling in of elements, the use of which is persistently denied, to eke out the scanty data of sense. Green proves that the relations are just as necessary and ultimate an element in experience as the so-called ultimate element (sensations or groups of sensations) of naturalism, and that every attempt to critically analyze experience, which ignores this formal side, is untrue to fact; and he shows, in particular, the consequences [16] of the national sensationalism, by exposing to view in the Prolegomena what results from the effort to carry this theory of fact out into the ethical universe. Indeed, eliminate the rational relations (categories), and the so-called experienced fact of naturalism is denuded of all meaning—it evaporates out of the world of real experience into nonentity. It is this insist-

---

[15] Hegel's Logic (Wallace) p. 77 ; cf. also Balfour's Foundations of Belief. p. 140.

[16] I am not thinking of consequences in the popular sense, as a test of truth See Prolegomena to Ethics, p. 10.

ence upon the necessary inherence of the categories in all experience, and their connexion with self-consciousness, that constitutes Kant's Copernican point of view and starts the philosophy of the century on its new line of discovery; and it is under the lead of the philosophy of Kant and his German successors that Green proceeds to his own philosophy of man and the world—of Experience.

What, then, is *experience?* What are its elements? All the travail of Green's metaphysics is involved in the answer. There is, perhaps, no better way of tentatively describing it in a few words, than by saying with Bradley, " that experience means something much the same as given and present fact . . . to be real, or even barely to exist, must be to fall within sentience. . . . We may say, in other words, that there is no being or fact outside of that which is commonly called psychical existence [17] . . . But to be utterly indivisible from feeling or perception, to be an integral element in a whole which is experienced, this surely is itself to *be* experience. Being and reality are, in brief, one thing with sentience; they can neither be opposed to, nor even in the end distinguished from it." [18] Whether experience in this sense is what is present merely to the finite consciousness is a question I propose to raise later. But whether it be this alone or ' more of the same kind ' we shall find that content of experience is the only intelligible conception of the Real which we can form. And this is easily seen from the contradiction into which any theory falls, which tries to find beyond experience a transcendent something which may exist out of all necessary relation to thought. [19] For, relation to thought is a *sine qua non* of all

---

[17] Bradley's App. and Reality, p. 145.

[18] Bradley's App. and Reality, p. 146.

[19] See Prolegomena, etc., p. 53:—" We can attach no meaning to ' reality ' as applied to the world of phenomena but that of existence under definite and unalterable relations ; and we find that it is only for a thinking consciousness, that such relations can subsist." See also Bradley's App. and Reality, p. 147 : " Anything, in no sense felt or perceived, becomes to me quite unmeaning. And as I cannot try to think of it without

existence, and to hold any other view is either to descend from philosophy to the particular sciences or to become the victim of a vicious abstraction. This is the true lesson of Kant's idealism, although Kant himself was never able to throw off the influence of the earlier dualism completely enough to see it in its fullness. And it makes no difference whether we are trying to think of this transcendent as mind or as matter, we come in either case to the same result. Nor do I know better how to put it than to say that we are asking thought to give us something which it cannot think, or asking experience to be experience of what cannot be experienced; and the special lesson to be learned from it is that the object, which experience reveals, is always thought's object, that is to say, is always object for a subject, and is not to be confused with matter considered as an external 'somewhat,' existing in its own right, apart from thought. To put this point in Green's own language—" It is important not to confuse the relation of subject and object with the relation of matter to the psychical organism. It is a common delusion that one sort of phenomena are 'subjective,' another 'objective.' In truth, 'mental phenomena' are just as objective as any, phenomena of matter just as subjective as any. If mind and matter=two orders of phenomena, they do not equal subject and object, for subject and object are correlative factors of everything as known." [20] The confusion of these two radically different relations is responsible for much of the contradiction in English philosophy from Locke to Spencer, and the resolution of the confusion constitutes the most noteworthy claim that modern idealism since Kant may make upon the gratitude of the thinking world. It is hardly too much to say that this was a fundamental illusion of philosophy from Descartes to the

realizing either that I am not thinking at all, or that I am thinking of it against my will as being experienced, I am driven to the conclusion that for me experience is the same as reality. The fact that falls elsewhere seems, in my mind, to be a mere word and a failure, or else an attempt at self-contradiction."

[20] Green's Works, Vol. II, pp. 181–182.

last quarter of the eighteenth century.   The origin of it is
not difficult to trace.   It arises from "taking common sense
as the guide of theory and not as its material."   According
to common sense, external things (the material world) exist
"apart in themselves just as I perceive them;" they constitute in themselves "a world of realities independent of any
mind to know them," [21] while the mind has an "equally complete and independent existence."   The problem of knowledge
then easily gets stated as the problem of bringing the two
opposites of subject and object together in the experience of
a world.   But it is easy to see that with two such independent opposites as these on our hands, there can be no rational
reconciliation, for the false statement of the problem has
already precluded the possibility of a solution.[22]   Nothing
then remains but the assertion of some miracle of Occasion-
alism or Pre-established Harmony, or an assertion of some
form of crude Realism or Dualism which satisfies itself with
"formulating the uncritical assumptions of the ordinary consciousness and re-stating in formal language as an ultimate
belief the hard opposition of mind and matter, thought and
things, in which common sense instinctively rests . . ." [23]
But how the character of the transcendent *thing* can be
reached or known by the mind which, on supposition, is
absolutely separate from it—this is a question to which none
of the forms of common sense theory can supply an answer
able to stand the light of criticism.   Doctrines of Pre-
established Harmony do not untie the knot, they simply cut
it; and the same is true of all forms of common-sense
Realism.   If taken seriously and driven to their logical issue,
they inevitably lead to agnosticism.   In Mr. Spencer's
'Psychology,' [24] the confusing conception of this relation of
subject and object is found in a statement which may well
be considered typical—"The relation between these, as

---

[21] J. Caird's Philosophy of Religion, p. 222.

[22] E. Caird's Critical Philosophy of Kant, pp. 13, sqq.

[23] John Caird, loc. cit., p. 223.   [24] Edition of 1872, § 387.

antithetically opposed divisions of the entire assemblage of manifestations of the unknowable, was our datum. The fabric of conclusions built upon it must be unstable if this datum can be proved either untrue or doubtful. Should the idealist be right, the doctrine of evolution is a dream." Now the aim of all the best idealistic thinking since Kant (that is, of all idealism which is not abstractly subjective) is simply in the interest of consistent thinking to show that the two are so strictly correlated, that neither is real if it be taken apart from the other; that "the determination of the one implies a corresponding determination of the other. The object, for instance, may be known, under one of the manifold relations which it involves, as matter, but it is only so known in virtue of what may indifferently be called a constructive act on the part of the subject, or a manifestation of itself on the part of the object . . . Nor is it to the purpose to say that, though matter *as known* involves the relation of subject and object, matter in itself does not. We need not inquire for the present into the meaning of 'matter in itself.' The matter which is in question, when we speak of a relation between mind and matter as equivalent to that between object and subject, is not 'matter in itself,' but matter as a 'phenomenon' or as known ; and since in this sense it is a certain sort of relation between object and subject, it may not be identified with one member of that relation to the exclusion of the other." [25] But the real difficulty with every such theory as that of Spencer (and his is only taken as typical) is that so far from rendering science (and along with science may be included the particular doctrine of Evolution) intelligible, it destroys the fundamental conditions on which science itself is ultimately based. Nor is there any conflict between this criticism and the demands of common sense, if it be understood that common sense furnishes to philosophy not theory — not final doctrine — but raw-material. Of course, common sense is justifiable when it makes its deliver-

[25] Green's Works, Vol. I, p. 387.

ance on the distinction between subject and object, but it certainly is not justifiable when, to satisfy the superficial requirements of its first attempts at reflective thinking, it hardens this distinction into the fixed opposition and independence of two mutually exclusive entities which it calls mind and matter.

It is this confusion which vitiates to the core Mr. Spencer's evolution philosophy. He has followed straight in the footsteps of common sense theory and misinterpreted the relation of subject and object, which is a valid distinction of all true philosophy, "into a 'dictum' on the part of consciousness that something independent of itself—something which can exist without consciousness, though not consciousness without it—is acting upon it; [26] and then proceeds to explain that knowledge of the world which is the developed relation between subject and object, as resulting from an action of one member of the relation upon the other. It ascribes to the object, which in truth is nothing without the subject, an independent reality, and then supposes it gradually to produce certain qualities in the subject, of which the existence is in truth necessary to the possibility of those qualities in the object which are supposed to produce them." [27] In other words, instead of taking subject and object as ideal moments or aspects of a unitary world, the reality of which is constituted by self-consciousness, subject and object are "segregated" into two complex batches of phenomena, with an interaction between them which can be described as nothing short of mechanical.

[26] See E. Caird's Evolution of Religion, Lecture V.

[27] Green's Work, Vol. I, p. 388 ; also p. 466. "To imagine an evolution of the self-conscious subject from the gathered experience of the sentient organism—an evolution of the unifying agent from that which it renders one—is the last form which the standing $\overset{\text{ʽ}}{\iota}\sigma\tau\epsilon\rho\text{o}\nu$ $\pi\rho\acute{o}\tau\epsilon\rho\text{o}\nu$ of empirical psychology has assumed." See also Sorley's Ethics of Naturalism : "The evolution of mind or self-consciousness out of experience is, therefore, not merely to be regarded as a problem too intricate for psychological analysis. It is a mistake to regard it as a possible problem at all ; for it attempts to make experience account for and originate the principles on which its own possibility depends."

And finally, by laying stress on the world of the object, the qualities of this world—which are, in point of fact, inconceivable except in relation to the subject—aided by the doctrine of hereditary transmission, are supposed to produce those categories, relations, or 'forms of synthesis' without which, indeed, we could not conceive of a world of things. Such a glaring *petitio principii* it would be hard, I imagine, to find surpassed in the pages of any other great thinker.[28] For it is nothing short of an attempt to prove the validity of what I may call the thought relations or categories, by a proof every step of which assumes them. It is not strange that a philosophy, of which such logic as this is a fundamental feature, should in the end assert the existence of ultimate reality, and then contradict itself by declaring it to be unknowable. Reality becomes too absurd to be known, or in Bradley's phrase, "too good to be known."

I have emphasized this conception of the relation of subject and object to experience, and so to reality, because without it the central truth of Green's metaphysic disappears. It is the guiding thread which he takes with him through all the labyrinthine windings of his polemic against the empiricists. It is also his guide through the sustained analysis and patient construction in the metaphysical portion of the Prolegomena. It appears at the very beginning of the first chapter on the Metaphysics of Knowledge (Book I),[29] in the exposition of the meaning of the question, 'Can the knowledge of nature be itself a part or product of nature'? This is not a question as to the relation between body and mind. The physiological psychologists may show the brain conditions of mind and explain certain relations of mind and matter in terms of psychophysical laws, but the true epistemological question will not have been touched, for the question is still unanswered—'How do we come to have these "objects of conscious-

---

[28] For a thorough discussion of this, see Green's Works, Vol. I, pp. 383 sqq.

[29] Prolegomena, etc., p. 13.

ness" called matter and motion'? And it is easily seen that matter and motion, so far from being an ultimate explanation of consciousness, themselves " consist in, or are determined by, relations between the objects of that connected consciousness which we call experience." No definition of matter, then, which abstracts from relations for which consciousness is a *sine qua non*, can be given, for when these relations disappear matter disappears along with them. And the same is true of motion. The object of consciousness—the experienced — can thus always be shown to be determined by relations. " . . . . . we shall try in vain to render an account to ourselves of position or succession, of a body or its identity, except as expressing relations of what is contained in experience, through which alone that content possesses a definite character and becomes a connected whole." [30]

The question arises, How does Green treat these relations, and what do they imply in order to their possibility ? Now it must be confessed that the incompleteness of Green's account of these thought relations,[31] which form such a prominent feature of his system, is a stumbling-block to his friends and a rock of offense to his critics. He gives no explicit classification indicating their connection one with another; they are given to us, as it were, 'in the lump'. It certainly seems strange that a philosophy so shot-through with thought-forms and categories and relations should have done so little, as one of his critics says, to " exhibit the inter-connection of these categories and trace them up to the highest principle, viz., Absolute Self-consciousness. . . . He nowhere enters upon a full discussion of the nature of these relations. His use of the single word ' relation ' would seem to indicate that, according to him, all relations are on the same level. An object — perhaps, to exactly

[30] Prolegomena, etc., p. 14.

[31] For a criticism of Green's doctrine, see Mind, April, '91. A. Eastwood : On Thought-Relations, pp. 243–252.

represent Green, we should say a feeling — is related to another object, and the objective world as a whole is related to the unity of self-consciousness. Are both the relations of the same kind and of the same value"?[32] Now while there is some truth in this criticism, it is still only a relative truth. For while it is true that Green has exhibited no graduated list of the categories, such as would show their relative value in enabling us to interpret the Real consistently, no Hegelian movement whereby we pass through the categories of *being*, which correspond to our earliest and most childlike understanding of the world, to those of *relation*, and through these again up to the categories of *ideal* and *organic unity*,—it is also true that there is nothing in the metaphysical doctrine of the Prolegomena to prevent us from saying that Green does recognize a difference in the ontological value of his 'relations'.[33] And so, for a reply to the criticism implied in Mr. Haldar's question, 'Are both the relations of the same kind and of the same value'? it is only necessary to turn to Green himself (p. 30, Prolegomena), where we read : " To suppose that this something else (self-consciousness), if nature (the one all-inclusive system of relations) were found unthinkable without it, is related to those conditions, of which the relation to each other forms the system of nature, in the same way in which these are related to each other, would no doubt be in contradiction with our account of this system as one and all-inclusive. It could not, therefore, be held to be related to them as, for instance, an invariable antecedent to an invariable sequent, or as one body to another outside it. But there would be no contradiction in admitting a principle which renders all relations possible, and is itself determined by none of them, if, on consideration of what is needed to constitute a system of relations, we found such a principle to

[32] Philosophical Review, June, '94' p. 172 ; Green and His Critics, by Prof. H. Haldar. Cf. also E. Caird's Critical Philosophy of Kant, Vol. II, p. 24.

[33] Green's attitude towards the ' dialectical ' method of Hegel—a critical attitude —may be seen on p. 146 of the third volume of his ' Works.'

be requisite." [34]   In other words, the relation of externality involved in such finite categories as those of succession and causal connexion cannot be applied to the universe, taken as a whole and determined by self-consciousness. And this is so because there is nothing external to self-consciousness; nothing to which it can be related in terms of succession or of causal dependence. [35]   To speak of self-consciousness as the presupposition of the order of relations which constitute experience, is a very different thing from speaking of the relation of one finite thing to another within the self-determined whole. Green is right in saying that it is absurd to speak of that, which is the condition of the relations, as being itself in relation. Failure to recognize this truth is largely responsible for that conception of a dualism of mind and matter, conceived as independent entities, which logical thinking is always driving to its implied skepticism. This confusion is best seen in the ordinary realistic assumption of the world of objects as external to consciousness, where the spatial relation of finite things to each other is forced into the doctrine that they exist *out* of that consciousness which is the condition of there being any such relation as space at all.

The next question, What do these relations imply? or What is the condition of their possibility? leads us into the very heart of Green's metaphysic. It is generally recognized

[34] The parentheses are mine.   Cf. also for a further statement —' Prolegomena to Ethics,' pp. 54–56.   This argument (used freely by Green), to wit, " that the ultimate evidence for the presence or action, of anything, lies in results inexplicable without it," Fairbrother strangely and perversely enough calls an argument from effect to cause, (Philosophy of T. H. Green, p. 14) ; see also A. J. Balfour's Defence of Philosophic Doubt, p. 94.

[35] This does not apply to cause in the sense of ' free-cause.' For this distinction, see Green's Prolegomena, etc., p. 81 ; cf. also Ormond's ' Basal Concepts of Philosophy,' where the dual nature of causality is emphasized—p. 73 :   " While causation says that every part of the series must have an antecedent condition, its deeper voice says also that in order to be completely explanatory, this condition must also include in it the creative ground of its being," and on p. 266 : " The idea of cause has coiled up in it the idea of self-activity and when this presupposition is drawn out, the idea of the world-ground is born."

that the answer to this question, which brings before us his doctrine of self-consciousness, is the central tenet of his system.[36] For just as sense-impressions, or in Green's language, feelings, have no reality except through their interpretation in a system of relations[37] so the relations are not self-sustaining and have no meaning when withdrawn from self-consciousness which is the only combining medium[38] or relating function which we directly know. It is, then, to an elaboration of a true doctrine as to the full and complete nature of such 'consciousness' that the metaphysical portion of the Prolegomena moves. Nor in his conception of the fundamental importance of such a doctrine is Green false to the spirit of the Kantian and post-Kantian idealism. For it may be said without exaggeration that since the Critique of Pure Reason, the problem of the Self has been *the* problem of philosophy. Modern philosophy, it is true, had, in its founder Descartes, tried to find in self-consciousness, in the thought of the thinker, some resting-place secure against the intrusion of doubt; but its conception of thought as a factor in the world was so abstract,[39] that the philosophy which was its logical successor, was forced in order to save the reality of the objective world to bring in a mediating principle in the form of a *Deus ex machina* — an infinite who is "brought in through a trap-door or is let down in a swing." Descartes' insight was a true one, but neither his genius nor the material of thought in the form of preceding systems or of surrounding culture, made it possible for him to see its full implications. When he says "I will question everything which I can doubt," he virtually or implicitly posits the 'I'

[36] Seth's Hegelianism and Personality, p. 3.

[37] Cf. Green's Works, Vol. I, p. 378 ; see also Prolegomena, etc., p. 125.—" We know nothing of self-consciousness apart from feeling, and are probably entitled to assume that there is no such thing, etc."

[38] Cf. Lotze's Outlines of Psychology, p. 94.

[39] Cf. E. Caird's Essays on Literature and Philosophy, Vol. II, Essay on Cartesianism ; also Royce's Studies in Good and Evil.—' The Implications of Self-consciousness,' pp. 146 sqq.

as the umpire by whose verdict everything is to be decided;[40]
in other words, he could not talk of questioning without im-
plying the criterion of self-consciousness—of reality—by
which the particular doubt as a fact of empirical consciousness gets a meaning for itself.   In the mere flow of states,
or rather, in the abstract existence of individual, isolated
states of the empirical consciousness—the Heraclitean flux of
feeling—there is no truth.[41]   For no state in its naked particularity (realizable as such, of course, only by the power of
abstraction which intelligence has), though the state be one
called doubt, can *mean* anything.   If then, it be taken as
referring to the Real, as *meaning* something, it can only get
that meaning by transcending the particularity of the moment
and becoming related to a wider consciousness of which it is
an organic element.[42]   When we leave empirical psychology
where states of consciousness are regarded in the abstract,
and pass to metaphysics, we may say that " in knowing, the
consciousness of each moment is significant of something
beyond itself, or rather gains significance because in knowing
we do not read it *qua* state of consciousness at all, but as a
member of an objective system of facts.   This is what is implied in the statement that knowledge is concerned with
ideas as meanings.   For in itself and in isolation, no idea
can have any meaning attaching to it at all.   Its significance
comes from its place or function as a member of a system." [43]
There is therefore neither ' rhyme nor reason ' in asking
whether any idea is real unless we are referring to "something other than the idea itself."   And the conclusion which
Green would draw from this is that only in a system of relations by which the nature of ideas is constituted, can be

[40] J. Caird's Spinoza (Blackwood's Classics) p. 95.

[41] Cf. Prolegomena, etc., p. 32.—" Feeling may be the revelation, etc."

[42] See J. Caird's Philosophy of Religion, on ' Ideal or Organic Universality,'
pp. 217 sqq.

[43] See J. E. Creighton's article, ' Is the Transcendental Ego an unmeaning conception ?' in Phil. Rev., March, '97 ; also Royce's Conception of God, pp. 141–181,
and Bradley's App. and Reality.

found a ground for distinguishing one idea as real and another
as unreal. In vol. 1, p. 153 (Green's Works) we read that
"an isolated idea could be neither real nor unreal. Apart
from a definite order of relations we suppose (if we like)
that it would *be*, but it would certainly not be real; and as
little could it be unreal, since unreality can only result from
the confusion in our consciousness of one order of relation
with another." If this be the true state of the case, we are
able to say that reality apart from thought is reality the
meaning of which cannot be conceived, for the very idea of
it is a contradiction,—a result which seems at first sight less
important than it really is. For to get rid of the notion that
the world can first exist as real in independence of thought[44]
and may afterwards be thought of — to see that it is meaningless to predicate existence of it except so far as it is an
object of thought—is to get in our possession "the only possible 'proof of the being of God', as the self-conscious subject"[45] without whose existence the world of nature and of
finite spirits would disappear. The argument, then, from
the existence of the finite object or from the multiplicity of
finite objects which are presented in the piecemeal and fragmentary experience of the finite individual as such, or better
still, the argument, to the existence of an infinite and eternal
self-consciousness, from the consciousness of man, is not an
argument from the finite determined as such to an external
ground or cause, but one which proceeds to show that the
finite loses all meaning except as it is conceived as a moment
in a fuller and self-determined whole. Or to put the thought
in the language of Edward Caird — "it is one thing to say
that from my thought I can argue to a reality which is supposed to be external to my thought and independent of it
and another thing to say that the distinction between my
thought and reality cannot be made except by a consciousness which in a sense embraces both."[46] By a misapprehen-

---

[44] See D. G. Ritchie's Darwin and Hegel, pp. 88–89.
[45] Green's Works, Vol. I, pp. 155–156.
[46] E. Caird's Critical Phil. of Kant, Vol. I, P. 114.

sion of this thought and consequently by a misinterpretation
of the main drift of Green's argument, Mr. Balfour, in his
Foundations of Belief,[47] finds the idealism of the Prolegomena
tainted by solipsism.   And another critic, who writes philosophy of a less popular and *ad captandum* type, has put
himself on record as unwilling to believe that Green's Infinite
and Eternal Consciousness is anything else than a ' hypos-
tatised abstraction.'[48]

The basis of Green's whole theory, according to Balfour, '' is a criticism or analysis of the essential elements of
experience.   But the criticism must, for each of us, be
necessarily of *his own* experience, for of no other experience
can he know anything, except indirectly and by way of
inference from his own.   What, then, is this criticism supposed to establish (say) for me?   Is it that experience
depends upon the unification by *a* self-conscious ' I ' of a
world constituted by relations ?   In strictness, No.   It can
only establish that *my* experience depends upon a unification
by *my* self-conscious ' I ' of a world of relations present to me
and to me alone.   To this ' I ', to this particular ' self-conscious subject,' all other ' I's', including God, must be objects . . . . '' [49]   But a criticism of this sort fails to
touch the essential feature of Green's theory, because of the
abstract way in which Mr. Balfour interprets the term
' experience'.   The whole question, I submit, turns on the
meaning to be given to the expression ' my experience'.
Who is this ' I ' ?[50]   And *how much* experience can it claim
as *its own?*   Recent psychology has been showing that the
concept of personality is a very complex concept, that the

<hr>

[47] Page 153.

[48] Seth's Hegelianism and Personality, Chap. I ; cf. D. G. Ritchie's criticism of
Seth in Mind, '88, p. 257.

[49] See Royce's Spirit of Modern Philosophy, p. 368 ; also Vol. IV, No. 5, Phil.
Rev., p. 478.—Here Royce gives an account of the necessity of going beyond what is
immediately presented in any state of consciousness to conceived possible experience,
in order to know what the immediately presented datum means.

[50] Cf. Watson's Outline of Philosophy, p. 186.

elements involved in it are far reaching, and that no account of it, which involves the hard and fast separation of the individual from the life of his fellows, is at all adequate.[51] So the whole drift of Green's argument is to show, through the analysis of what is involved in any fact or series of facts, the implications of the consciousness which is pre-supposed. And when Mr. Balfour asserts that of ' no other experience can he know anything, except indirectly and by way of inference from his own ', it is a legitimate retort that he does not in strict logic know even his own except indirectly and by way of inference.[52] Moreover, he does not come to know his own at all, from the standpoint of the phenomenology of consciousness, except as a contrast effect over against the consciousness of his fellows. '' Those who have begun philosophy by saying ' The self at least is known,' have usually forgotten that the self as known is at the outset neither the empirical Ego of the world of common sense, nor yet merely the so-called ' self of the one present moment.' It is not the first because philosophy has not yet at the outset come to comprehend the world of common sense. It is not the second, for the consciousness of the ' present moment ' can only be defined in relation to a reflection that transcends the present moment; whilst on the other hand, no human reflection has ever yet fathomed perfectly the consciousness of even a single one of our moments.'' [53]

---

[51] Baldwin's recent work.—' Social and Ethical Interpretations,' is probably the best in the language on this subject. See also Alexander's Moral Order and Progress, pp. 89 sqq.

[52] See Bradley's App. and Reality, pp. 255–258, on the contradictory character of Solipsism ; also J. H. Muirhead on the ' Goal of Knowledge,' Mind, Oct., '97, p. 491 : '' But no argument can be brought in support of the view that the existence of other minds is hypothetical which would not apply equally *mutatis mutandis* to the existence of our own. Here, as in the the case of subject and object in general, it is better to say that ' others' consciousness ' is one of the factors which the analysis of self-consciousness yields to the psychologist, ' our consciousness ' being the other. They thus stand on the same level of immediacy. for neither is really immediate at all.'' See also Royce's articles in Phil. Rev., Sept., '95, p. 471, and Sept., '94, p. 532, and Bradley's App. and Realty, pp. 248 sqq.

[53] Royce, Studies in Good and Evil, p. 155.

There is, then, no justification for the assertion that the 'experience' which furnishes the point of departure for Green's construction is the mere isolated subject, which a subjective idealism hypostatises. It is instead the experience which expresses itself in the fact: "Something is real,"[54] proceeding then by a process of analysis and inference to unfold the full meaning of the assertion, and finding as a final result, when philosophy has pushed its examination as far as it can, that all fact and knowledge of fact presuppose the existence of an eternal and all-inclusive self-distinguishing consciousness. And this final result is no more reached by a mere 'leap' than the knowledge of the true meaning of 'my self-conscious I' is to be *assumed* as given all at once as a brute fact. For if one were now to say that his personal self or soul were the only datum clearly known to him, that all else, including the non-ego, were vague and uncertain, that he could know nothing but his own subjective states, we might rightly say of him that he was still stating the problem of knowledge in the form given it by Descartes, and had failed to avail himself of the lesson of post-Kantian idealism. That idealism says, and rightly says, that you only learn the true meaning of your finite selfhood by reflection; that the knowledge of it is not simply *given*, and that through reflection the finite self gets to know itself with a deepening insight, only as it gets contrasted with some wider self of more fully organized expericuce, which transcends while at the same time it includes it. Instead, then, of saying with Balfour that the movement of Green's thought as a 'criticism or analysis of the essential elements of experience' leads to solipsism, we may say that the solipsism, which he finds, results from a misinterpretation of the meaning of the 'experience' on which

[54] Royce, Conception of God, p. 207. Cf. Green's Works, Vol. III, 'The Philosophy of Aristotle,' p. 74.—". . . the minimum of knowledge, which can form a beginning of conscious experience, may be expressed as the judgment, 'something is.'" See also McTaggart's Studies in Hegelian Dialectic, Chap. II.

the Neo-Kantian or Neo-Hegelian idealism is supposed to be based. [55]

It is this abstract way of interpreting 'experience' that lies at the basis of his criticism (cf. Foundations, etc., pp. 156–157) of Professor Caird's proof for the existence of God in his 'Evolution of Religion.' "Surely," he says, "we must think of God as, on the transcendental theory, we think of ourselves; that is, as a Subject distinguishing itself from, but giving unity to, a world of phenomena. But if such a Subject and such a world cannot be conceived without also postulating some higher unity in which their differences shall vanish and be dissolved, then God Himself would require some yet higher deity to explain His existence." [56] Such a criticism loses its meaning as soon as it is seen that this higher unity is not a unity which lies beyond or outside of the lower, but one which brings out the implications of the lower, and shows that its imperfections can be reconciled only through the conception of an infinite and self-determined whole. " . . . . . the consciousness of self and the consciousness of God are essentially bound up with each other." [57] For the experience in which the finite subject and the multiplicity of finite objects are the two complementary sides is forever showing its incompleteness by falling into contradiction with itself through error and illusion; and it is the consciousness of this limitation [58] which forever drives it out of itself and puts before it the ideal of a wider and more completely organized experience, in

[55] For Green's own fear of subjective idealism, see his review of J. Caird's ' Introduction to the Philosophy of Religion,' Green's Works, Vol. III, p. 143.

[56] Foundations, etc., p. 157.

[57] E. Caird's Critical Philosophy of Kant, Vol. I, p. 215 ; cf. also Ormond's Basal Concepts, etc., p. 129 ; and J. Caird's Spinoza, p. 102.

[58] Hegel's Logic (Wallace) p. 116.--" No one knows, or even feels, that anything is a limit or defect, until he is at the same time above and beyond it." See also Green's Works, Vol. III, p. 86 ; Schurman's Belief in God, p. 23 ; E. Caird's Essays on Literature and Philosophy, Vol. II, p. 475. Expressions of this sort are constantly recurring in writers of the Neo-Hegelian type. A criticism by James may be found in his ' Will to Believe,' pp. 283, etc.—not at all convincing however.

which error and illusion, doubt and ignorance shall be done away.

This thought has been recently worked out with great felicity of phrase and subtlety of analysis by Professor Royce in his ' Conception of God.' [59] In reaching truth on the basis of Royce's contrast between a narrower and a wider experience—in other words, in appealing as I do in the sciences, from one grade of experience to another—I am continually appealing to the experience of my social fellows. The wider and more richly-organized experience to which I am appealing for the purpose of rendering valid or invalid any fact of my own relatively contracted sensible experience, is simply the vast systematic body of laws, conceptions and principles reached, as we say, on the basis of the verdict of the consensus of experts. But then these experts, taken as individuals or groups of individuals, have themselves a fragmentary, piecemeal experience, although it may be less fragmentary and less piecemeal than my own. I am, therefore, logically bound to estimate and to put limits about their experience in terms of an experience still wider. Indeed, nothing but an absolute experience can satisfy my search for the criterion of truth. Reality, then, would be what the Absolute Thinker—one in whom there is no lack of completeness—experiences " in one time-transcending moment." [60] If this be so, we are bound to recognize that the experience which philosophy interprets is first given in a relatively undifferentiated form, and that it is the

[59] Page 34.

[60] See J. Caird's Phil. of Religion, pp. 144 sqq. for a discussion of the Ontological argument ; also E. Caird's Critical Philosophy, etc., Vol. II, Chap. XIII and Evolution of Religion, Vol. I, Lectures V and VI ; Ormond's Basal Concepts, etc., Chap. XVII. See also Royce's Conception of God, pp. 30, etc. : For an answer to the question—' Is this ideal unity more than a bare possibility ? '—see Royce, pp. 36 sqq ; Here and elsewhere in this work, Royce unfolds the implications of ' possible experience.' Cf. Mill's Examination of Sir Wm. Hamilton's Philosophy, Vol. I, Chaps. XI and XII, also Balfour's Defence of Philosophic Doubt, Chap. IX, Ritchie's Darwin and Hegel, p. 104, E. Caird's Essays, etc., Vol. II, p. 475, and Royce's Spirit of Modern Philosophy, pp. 430 sqq.

business of the philosopher to analyze it and tell what it means. Through judgment which becomes more and more explicit and precise, this relatively undifferentiated unity is differentiated into a multiplicity of things and souls which are interpreted by common sense as existing in a distinct and independent way and external to each other. But the same differentiating thought, which expresses itself in our earlier and more inadequate judgments, is seen by a more thorough-going reflection, to carry in itself a function of integration.[61] The earlier unity which thought rends asunder in its process of acquiring knowledge, passes over into a higher unity, in which the conflict and opposition of the lower stage are reconciled in a richer conception of reality. And this applies to the highest unity, which Caird calls God. His is not a unity which excludes or exists alongside of another, in some external way, but one which includes and reconciles within its perfect self-deter-mination all the hard oppositions and conflicting contrasts which are so pressing a feature of our finite and conse-quently imperfect self-consciousness. When, therefore, it is said that "in Him, we live and move and have our being," we are not dealing with a phrase expressive merely of pious mysticism, but with a thought which is the result of man's deepest reflection into the presuppositions of his life.[62]

This interpretation throws light upon one of the con-stantly recurring criticisms of a theory like Green's—the criticism that it destroys the validity of the objective world and tends to reduce our supposed common sense knowledge of such a world to a species of illusionism. This is, of course, the easy criticism of any theory of reality which may happen to be called idealistic. But whatever result the logic of

---

[61] See H. Jones' Philosophy of Lotze, pp. 359, etc., for a more complete statement of this thought ; also J. Watson's Christianity and Idealism, pp. 13S sqq.

[62] Cf. Royce's Religious Aspect of Philosophy, Chap. XI, also his Conception of God, pp. 343, etc.

Green's system may, in the minds of his critics, be driven to, it was surely no thought of his own mind, that to this issue it was tending. On the contrary, the whole of his criticism of the empiricists has, as its underlying purpose, the vindication of the existence of the external world of common sense.[63] He believed that there was no other method, except that of an idealism which proceeded along lines in some way similar to his own, for making this vindication secure. Common sense says that "things affect each other, but the mere presence and absence of our perception does not affect them" and common sense is undoubtedly right. It treats things "as being when unapprehended by our minds, just the same as when apprehended by our minds." "Objective = independent of our consciousness for practical purposes,"— this is the first crude unreflective definition of what we mean when we speak of the externality of a world of objects.[64] Idealism so far agrees with common sense. But it does not agree with the meaning which unsophisticated common sense theorizes into this deliverance of consciousness, when it first begins to reflect. All the deliverances of consciousness are valuable to philosophy but they are not sacred merely because they are *given*. Metaphysics cannot afford to ignore common sense but neither can it afford to neglect to transcend it. Nor in this respect does it differ so very seriously from science. The truth of the matter is that common sense is *meaning* a truth but just because it is common or unsophisticated sense, it doesn't know how to express it, and easily falls into error when it enters upon the task of giving reasons. Lord Mansfield's oft-quoted advice to the Governor without legal training compelled to preside in a Colonial Court of Justice is specially applicable to it —

[63] I presuppose here the distinction found in Bosanquet's Essentials of Logic, pp. 8, 9, 10, between 'common sense' and 'common sense theory.'

[64] Cf. Royce's 'Conception, etc.,' pp. 144–181, for the idealistic implications contained in the 'realistic' concept of 'reality;' also his Spirit of Modern Philosophy, pp. 358, etc. ; and Bosanquet's Essentials, etc., Lectures I and II. See also Riehl's Introduction to the Theory of Science and Metaphysics, Part II, Chap. I, pp. 123–166.

" Give your decision boldly for it will probably be right but never venture on assigning reasons for they will almost infallibly be wrong." Among many similar statements scattered through his collected works, I take the following as an indication of Green's conception of the relation of idealism to the common sense notion of reality,[65] taken in what I may call its 'first intention': "The fact that there is a real external world of which through feeling we have a determinate experience, and that in this experience all our knowledge is implicit, is one which no philosopher disputes. The idealist merely asks for a further analysis of a fact which he finds so far from simple."[66] Again, "the true question is not whether there is such a thing as external matter, but what it is external to; whether its outwardness is an outwardness *to* thought, or an outwardness of body to body only—possible *for* thought."[67] Green would say that the pressing duty of any philosopher, in search of a true theory of reality, is to keep himself free from the confusion of thinking that the relation of thought to its object is the same as the relation of externality of one material thing to another in the world of space;[68] free from the error of translating "'subject' and 'object' straight away into the (supposed) definite individual soul and the (supposed) real world of ordinary thought, which is so largely impregnated with the traditional dualistic philosophy. If we start with the assertion of an absolute difference between the soul as thinking substance and matter as the opposite kind of substance, no wonder if we find a difficulty in explaining the possibility of knowledge .... A very slight amount of careful thinking shows us that the 'soul' and the 'thing' are alike mental constructs, inferences,

---

[65] See Ritchie's Darwin and Hegel, pp. 77–105 ; also Royce's Studies in Good and Evil, pp. 156–162, for different meanings of the expression 'external object.'

[66] Green's Works, Vol. I, p. 376, Vol. III, p. 49 ; Royce's Spirit of Modern Philosophy, p. 382.

[67] Works, Vol. I, p. 380 ; see also Ferrier's Institutes of Metaphysics, p. 105.

[68] D. G. Ritchie's ' Darwin and Hegel,' pp. 88, 89, 90.

not primitive data of consciousness." [69]   Not to make this distinction in the present day is to show one's self unqualified to undertake the task of philosophical analysis at the Kantian point of view.   It was Kant's imperfect grasp of his own better insight on this point that led him, despite the logic of his own theory, to put behind experience, as the cause of the raw material of sense, an unknowable world of ' things in themselves'. But according to Green, this " crude notion of the antithesis between what is real and what is thought gives way before the consideration that all reality lies in relations and that only for a thinking consciousness do relations exist." [70]   And to those who charge him with ignoring the reality which they suppose to belong to feeling and matter, and giving the world over to a realm of static abstract thought, an answer may be found in the words which I now quote—" It is apt to be supposed that reality in some special sense belongs (a) to feeling, as that which the individual cannot help having, (b) to what is material.   But the supposition (a) in fact means that the feeling is real in virtue of its *relation to an outward cause*, and for a merely feeling consciousness there would be no such relation. Feelings being successive, there could be no identification of one with another (in the judgment ' this that I now feel is the same object that I felt before '), no reference of feeling to an outward cause which does not pass along with it.   We must always bear in mind that when certain writers speak of the ' unreality of mere feeling,' they mean feeling as it would be for a merely feeling consciousness. Every feeling has abundant reality as determined by its actual conditions and effects; but what is meant is that for a subject that merely felt there would not be this determination (this determination would not be presented as an object)." [71]

---

[69] Phil. Review, Vol. III, No. 1, p. 27.—Ritchie on ' The Relation of Metaphysics to Epistemology.'

[70] Works, Vol. II, p. 177.

[71] Works, Vol. II, p. 177.—' The Logic of the Formal Logicians.'

Again, what shall we say of the reality which is supposed to belong to the material world—to what Mr. Balfour calls (Foundations of Belief, p. 147) 'the world of objects'? Shall we say, or rather does Green say or imply, that thought creates or produces it in a causal or quasi-causal way? Balfour seems to think that he does,[72] and claims that in so doing he violates the essential principles on which transcendental idealism is based. Now it is no doubt true that to 'invest the thinking self' with a productive function of this sort would be a violation of the true idealistic method. For that method ignores, and rightly ignores, the frivolous and absurd question as to 'how being is made.' Taking experience as it is, the business of that method is, not to ask how experience "came into being," "but moving always within the fact, it asks what are the conditions of its being what it is, what, in other words, are its essential elements." . . . . . the procedure of a transcendental philosophy, which would be consistent with itself, must be immanent throughout."[73] But Green expressly warns us (Prolegomena, p. 57) that any language which would seem to imply that the subject which is implied in the connexion of phenomena in the system of the world of nature, "is a cause of which nature is the effect," or "a substance of which the changing modes constitute nature," must be used, if at all, only on a clear understanding of its metaphorical character. The passage in which he unfolds his thought on this point is so important and so often ignored by his critics that I propose to give it in full. Supposing it granted, he says, that all reality lies in relations, there is still another doctrine harder to accept, viz., that "only for a thinking

---

[72] In Mind, Jan., '84, p. 80, and in the Foundations of Belief, p. 144, he says, indeed, that Green's method and principles make it "as correct to say that nature makes mind as that mind makes nature ; that the world created God as that God created the world." Seth agrees with him—see Hegelianism and Personality, p. 24.

[73] Seth's Hegelianism and Personality (First edition) p. 16.

consciousness do relations exist."[74]   But "the objections which suggest themselves to the doctrine that relations are constituted by thought do not apply to the doctrine itself (which, once understood, is irrefutable), but to its supposed implications. (a) What, according to it, becomes of 'external matter,' which all the exact sciences suppose ? The answer is, that it is unaffected by the doctrine, except that externality has to be understood as of *matter* to *matter*, not of matter to thought ; 'matter' and 'externality' alike meaning certain relations which thought constitutes. (b) Is there then nothing other than thought ? . . . . . We answer to (b): undoubtedly there is something other than thought. Feeling is so; the whole system of nature, on which |feeling depends, is so; its otherness from thought makes it what it is; but this is the same as saying that relation to thought makes it what it is; that but for thought it would not be. Conversely, 'otherness' from nature makes thought what it is.   The very idea of thought implies a ἕτερον, for thought = self-consciousness or consciousness of the distinction between subject and object, and thought cannot be conscious of itself except in distinction from an object. . . . Subject and object, thought and its ἕτερον, are correlative or complementary factors in the whole of self-consciousness, or (which is the same) together constitute the unity of the world.   Each is what it is *in relation* to the other; but there is this difference, that whereas it is true to say that only *for* the subject or *for* thought is the object or the ἕτερον what it is, it is not true to say that only for the object or for the ἕτερον is the subject or thought what it is (just because the *for* implies relation to consciousness, and the ἕτερον is that, in the whole formed by self-consciousness, which is not conscious)."

In connection with this thought which I have just been discussing, it is held by some critics that Green's idealism militates against the scientific fact of the world's reality

[74] Works, Vol. II, p. 179.

previous to the appearance of thinking beings.[75]   According to them the objective world would have to come into existence when A, B, or C, begins to think.   But I think it is evident that such an interpretation as this is nothing short of a travesty, significant not of a defect in the idealism which is supposed to support it, but of an inability or refusal on the part of the critic to make the distinction between a purely subjective idealism and the critical and objective idealism of Kant and his successors.   Such an interpretation runs counter to the fundamental doctrine of Green's metaphysics wherever you find it, whether in the positive and constructive form in which it appears in the Prolegomena or in the critical writings of his other works.   That fundamental doctrine is the ultimate nature of Thought as an infinite and eternal self-conscious principle.   The true meaning of the personality of man is found when we see that "in the process of our learning to know the world, an animal organism, which has its history in time, gradually becomes the vehicle of an eternally complete consciousness.   'Our consciousness' may mean either of two things; either a function of the animal organism, which is being made gradually and with interruptions, a vehicle of the eternal consciousness; or that eternal consciousness itself,[76] as making the

[75] For an example, see The New World, of March, '92' p. 157. Cf. also Kuno Fisher's Kant, pp. 15 sqq ; H. Jones' Philosophy of Lotze, p. 367 ; A. Eastwood in Mind, Oct. '92' p. 485 ; Schiller's Riddles of the Sphinx, p. 305 ; Bradley's App. and Reality, pp. 274-275.

[76] For criticism of Green's doctrine of the timeless self, see Seth's Man's Place in the Cosmos, p. 214 ; J. L. McIntyre on Time and the Succession of Events, Mind, July, 1895 ; Schiller on The Metaphysics of the Time-Process, Mind, Jan., 1895. For further literature on this important point (which I am sorry to leave undiscussed in this paper) see the bibliography at the close. Royce's Conception of God and Spirit of Modern Philosophy (Part II) are suggestive on the relation of Time to the Absolute ; and so too is McTaggart's Studies in Hegelian Dialectic.   Cf. also Ormond's Basal Concepts, etc., Chap. IV (Space and Time) pp. 59-69, and Lotze's Metaphysics, Vol. I, Book II, Chap. III.   On the relation of the human soul to the Absolute, see Ormond's Basal Concepts, etc., pp. 197, 258, etc ; and E. Caird's Critical Philosophy, etc., Vol. I, p. 424 ; also D. G. Ritchie in the Phil. Rev., Jan.' '94' p. 28.   Bradley (App. and Reality) calls the timeless self a 'psychological monster: suppose it be granted, do we still have to say that it is a metaphysical monster ?

animal organism its vehicle and subject to certain limitations in so doing, but retaining its essential characteristic as independent of time, as the determinant of becoming, which has not and does not itself become."[77] According to Green it would not be necessary to believe that the world of nature comes into existence when A, B, or C, begins to think, unless it be "necessary to suppose that intelligence first comes into existence when this person or that begins to understand."[78] Or again, in a noteworthy passage (Works, vol. II, p. 73) — "The answer is that it is not our sentience that is the condition of there being for us a phenomenal world, though the fact that we are sentient (and, so far, merely parts of this world) limits (renders inadequate) the mode in which we understand it, *i. e.*, in which it exists as a phenomenal world for us. The conditions of there being for us such a world is the existence of a reason, which we call ours, but which we cannot suppose, without hopeless contradiction and confusion, to have begun with our sentient life . . . . . . (p. 74). The antecedent conditions of life and sentience . . . . . are conditions of what we experience, determined just as much by relation to what we experience, as it by relation to them. Limit 'our experience' to the succession of our feelings, and there is no 'world of experience'. Extend it to mean that which determines our feeling, and it must in elude conditions antecedent to the appearance of sentient life just as much as any other. If 'science' reveals such conditions, the right inference to draw is, not that the world is independent of thought, but that thought, the condition of there being such conditions, does not come into being as a development of life and sentience." In the face of such statements as these, the criticism mentioned above seems to be rendered null and void, if we suppose Green's central principle to be capable of logical justification. But this is

---

[77] Prolegomena, etc., pp. 72, 181, 189. For the genesis of this doctrine of Green, see Mind, Jan., 1890, pp. 73-74. Cf. also Bradley's App. and Reality, p. 226.

[78] Prolegomena, etc., p. 38. See also Works, Vol. II, pp. 182 and 80.

just the supposition which many of Green's critics say is an illogical superinduction on his premisses and the legitimate inferences from these. They claim that he has wrested Kant's transcendental 'unity of apperception' from its legitimate function and has made of the mere epistemological Ego something metaphysically real — in other words, that he has 'hypostatized an abstraction'. We are told that in Kant's system "the transcendental self, as the implicate of all experience, is for the theory of knowledge, simply the necessary point of view from which the universe can be unified,"[79] but that Green, in working out his theory along Kantian lines (cf. Seth, p. 20), has identified this self of epistemology with the universal or Divine self-consciousness and so has transformed "Kant's theory of knowledge into a metaphysic of existence, an absolute philosophy (Seth, p. 21)," and the implication is that he has fallen into error in so doing. This is, of course, a possibility, but there is certainly another alternative and that alternative is, that when Kant's contradictory doctrine of 'things in themselves' had been purged out of his system,[80] the transforma-

---

[79] Essays in Philosophical Criticism (Ed. by Seth and Haldane) p. 38 ; also Hegelianism and Personality, (Seth) p. 20 ; J. S. Mackenzie on Bradley's View of the Self, in Mind, July, '94 (especially p. 314). See also Green's Works, Vol. II, p. 24 sqq. For the distinction between the empirical and transcendental ego, see Seth's Hegelianism and Personality, pp. 14, 15. See Prolegomena, etc., p. 104, for an important passage in this connection : "If we are told that the Ego or Self is an abstraction from the facts of our inner experience—something which we 'accustom ourselves to suppose' as a basis or substratum for these, but which exists only logically, not really, —it is a fair rejoinder, that these so-called facts, our particular feelings, desires, and thoughts, are abstractions, if considered otherwise than as united in the character of an agent who is an object to himself." Cf. also Falckenberg's History of Modern Philosophy (Armstrong's trans.) pp. 349–354 ; Erdmann's History of Philosophy, Vol. II, pp. 378–380 ; Watson's Kant and his English Critics,' pp. 78-80 ; E. Caird's Hegel pp. 192–193.

[80] Prolegomena, etc., pp. 40 sqq. Mr. Balfour in his Foundations, etc., (pp. 144–145) shows that his thinking is still ridden by Pre-Kantian dualism, when he insists on a 'refractory element' in experience —'points between which the thought-relations may hold,' or at least that he has not got rid of one form of the thing-in-itself doctrine. See Lotze's Microcosmus, Book VIII, Chap. 1, p. 354. for "insoluble individual nuclei in the flux of thought." For a refutation of Balfour's position, consult

tion of his abstract conception of the unity of self-consciousness, as a merely formal unity, became not only a possibility
but a logical necessity.[81]   It was the work of Kant's genius
to point out with a suggestiveness which had never before
been equaled, that the unity of the Ego is a fundamental
condition of all experience; that the existence of all that we
know is existence for *thought*.   But his theory of knowledge
has also another side.   He denied "that that which exists
for our thought is absolute reality, a denial which again
involves the presence to our thought of an ideal of knowledge, by which our actual knowledge is condemned.   This
ideal, however, was falsely conceived by Kant as an identity
without any difference, and in this sense, he does not hesitate
to apply it even to self-consciousnes itself."[82]   Of the Ego,
Kant says, "we cannot even say that it is a concept, but
merely a consciousness that accompanies all concepts.   By
this I, or he, or it (the thing), which thinks, nothing is
represented beyond a transcendental subject of thoughts =
x, which is known only through the thoughts that are its
predicates, and of which, apart from them, we can never
have the slightest concept, so that we are really turning
round it in a perpetual circle, having already to use its
representation, before we can form any judgment about it.
And this inconvenience is really inevitable, because consciousness in itself is not so much a representation, distinguishing a particular object, but really a form of representation
in general, in so far as it is to be called knowledge, of which
alone I can say that I think something by it."[83]   But it is

Watson's Christianity and Idealism, pp. 121-152 ; also his Kant and his English
Critics, Chap. I.   See also Green's Works, Vol. III, pp. 149 sqq ; A. Eastwood,
Mind, April, 1891, 'On Thought-relations,' and Mind, April, 1894.—' Mr. Balfour's
Refutation of Idealism.'   For Lotze's position cf. McTaggart's Studies in Hegelian
Dialectic, pp. 117-118 ; Jones' Phil. of Lotze, pp. 342-343 ; McGilvary, Phil. Rev.,
Sept. '97' p. 501,—' The Presupposition Question in Hegel's Logic.'

[81] Cf. Morris' Kant (Grigg's Philosophical Classics) pp. 121-131 ; also Royce's
Spirit of Modern Philosophy, Appendix B.

[82] E. Caird's Essays on Literature and Philosophy, Vol. II, p. 431.

[83] Kant's Critique of Pure Reason (Max Müller's trans.) p. 282.

just this conception of "pure identity" as the 'ideal of knowledge' which forces Kant to "seek for absolute truth in a region beyond the objective consciousness." In the passage quoted, his own language shows that self-consciousness cannot be conceived as simple identity; "for if so, it must be purely an object or purely a subject, but really it is both in one; all things are *for it*, but it is *for itself*."[84]

It remained for Kant's successors to break down this conception of the purely logical or abstract unity of the Ego and to bring to light the true implications of the difference he draws between the *empirisches* and the *transcendentales Bewusstsein*, to show that the distinction he himself was forced to make by the necessities of his thinking between mere subjective personality and the *objektive Einheit des Bewusstseins* was a distinction which pointed logically to "the further universalizing of this human self-hood into the notion of the world-self of objective idealism,—the highest and deepest result of all modern philosophy";[85] to the trans-formation of his abstract unity of apperception into the principle of absolute self-consciousness. And it is in the line of this development that we find Green's conception of an universal and eternally complete Self as the foundation of his metaphysics—no mere hypostasis of an abstraction but a genuine attempt to solve a genuine problem.[86]

---

[84] For a discussion of this point, see E. Caird's Hegel, pp. 146-148. Cf. also E. Caird's essay on Metaphysics in his Essays on Lit. and Phil., Vol. II, for the development from Kant to Hegel ; and Seth's—"From Kant to Hegel." For a criticism of Kant's 'Transcendental Ego' and the Ego of the later idealists (including Green) cf. James' Psychology, Vol. I. pp. 360-370. An *ex cathedra* demolition (?) of Green by G. S. Fullerton may be found in the Psychological Review for July, '97.

[85] Royce's Spirit of Modern Philosophy, p. 487. Cf. also Caird's Critical Phil., etc., Vol. I, Book I, Chap. IV, 'The Transcendental Deduction of the Categories ;' and Vol. II, pp. 630-640; also Essays on Lit. and Phil., Vol. II, pp. 424, etc ; Adamson's Fichte, p. 136 ; Seth's 'From Kant to Hegel,' pp. 13, 28, 29, 30 ; W. Wallace, Lectures and Essays on Natural Theology and Ethics, pp. 39-41.

[86] In addition to the important passages in the first hundred pages of the Prolegomena, see also Green's Works, Vol. II, pp. 23-34 (especially sections 25 and 26). Cf. Dewey on Green's reconstruction of Kant, in his article in Mind, Jan., '90.

II.

I have said that when Kant's contradictory doctrine of
'things in themselves' had been purged out of his theory,
the transformation of his abstract conception of the unity of
consciousness, as a merely formal unity, became not only a
possibility but a logical necessity; and I have implied that
Green's Eternal Spiritual Principle is the ultimate result of
this transformation.   But assertion is not evidence and between it and belief or conviction evidence is necessary.   In
the negative vindication of Green as against his critics, we
have seen the importance attaching to his use of what I may
call the Divine Self, as the presupposition of knowledge.
We have seen that the analysis of any fact or matter of fact
has revealed its nature as consisting in relations and we have
also seen that the only medium, sustainer or source of relations is Thought.   We may grant then, that thought is the
source of the relations in terms of which the manifold of
sense becomes a phenomenal world of order and unity, but
the question arises — Whose thought?   Is it thought subjective and abstract or thought objective and concrete ?
Or again, are the relations, which thought mediates, of subjective or objective application, and does the distinction between subjective and objective application furnish a ground
for the further distinction between a cosmos of intelligible
objects as the only knowable world for us and a further
world of unknown 'things in themselves' separated from the
former world by a breach which no thought of ours can
mediate ?   According to Kant it is no doubt true that the
idea of the Self as an absolute unity is merely a regulative
idea, and the argument upon which he bases his doctrine is
drawn from the "assumption that the determining subject
cannot be made an object for itself, but as known is merely
a phenomenon."[87]   But if there be good reason for believ-

<hr>

[87] John Watson, An Outline of Philosophy, p. 428,

ing that the distinction between the world of experience and the world of 'things in themselves' is an invalid one, leading to self-contradiction and confusion, we are at once in possession of knowledge which makes it possible to see that the distinction made between the Self as a formal unity and the self as ontologically real is one which may no longer hold. The universalizing and absolutizing of the Kantian Unity of Apperception in post-Kantian idealism proceeds, indeed, *pari passu*, with the breaking down of this absolute distinction between the phenomenal world and the world of 'things in themselves'. Kant interprets self-consciousness " as nothing but a 'formal' or 'logical' aspect or condition of sensible consciousness. For him the conditioned product is the main thing. The conditioning process and *agency* is merely an ontologically insignificant incident of the former. This is wholly unintelligible and is in direct contradiction of the facts which Kant discovers and declares. Kant finds and declares the self-conscious activity, which conditions sensible consciousness, to be a 'pure activity', a 'pure spontaneity' of mind: it is livingly efficient, synthetic, organizing. It *does* something. It is the condition of all conscious doing and being. To assert, then, that it is after all only formal and logical and is *per se* only an insubstantial incident of sensible consciousness, or of the dependent product of its activity, is to use words which not only contradict the facts, as he finds and asserts them, but are devoid of meaning. As well might you say that the organizing forces which build up the tree are only 'incidental' or only 'logically' necessary to the tree regarded as a completed product . . . . . ." [88]

If we were to ask, then, for the origin of this doctrine as to the existence of a world outside of thought, we should find upon careful consideration that it results from an idealistic interpretation of the analysis of experience which, while it is victorious over the ordinary forms of common sense dualism, has still only an imperfect grasp on the principle

[88] Morris' Kant, pp. 122, 123.

which makes such a victory possible. It is idealism which is successful as criticism but which breaks down in its efforts to give an ultimate and positive construction of reality.[89] This characterization is true of it wherever you find it and Kant's Critique is only a special example: for victorious as this is over the skepticism, which first roused him from his dogmatic slumber, and so victorious too, over the dualistic assumptions the logical evolution of which had driven knowledge into such skepticism as into an absolute *cul de sac*, it yet fails in its own theory as to the ultimate nature of the real. With the true principle of knowledge in its hands,—that principle which Kant himself thought enough of to believe that in his hands it would effect a Copernican revolution in philosophy,—with its eyes fixed in the direction of the promise-land where thought would know reality and reality would be seen to be a contradiction if it were anything else than intelligible, it waveringly fails " to overcome the separation which in our ordinary thinking we assume, between the faculty or capacity or subjective process of experience on the one side and the facts experienced on the other."[90] It failed to work out to its final conclusion the only result which any thorough-going analysis of fact and knowledge of fact can support,—the result that thought and all the data which thought mediates can exist only as combined in one whole of experience. The result then, which Kant reaches, is the altogether absurd one that there are two worlds—on the one hand, the world of our knowledge and experience, a world characterized by the orderly connexion of its phenomenal contents and about which intelligible predication is possible; on the other, a world of unknowable 'things in themselves,' in theory absolutely divorced from the former, but in actual practice, owing to the absurdity of its isolation, ever and anon forcing itself into relationship with it in terms of some category the applica-

---

[89] Cf. Royce's Conception, etc.—Supplementary Essay.

[90] Prolegomena to Ethics, p. 36.

bility of which Kant's theory has already rendered untenable. This world of 'things in themselves' is supposed to exist, but what its character is we are supposed to be utterly unable to say. But such a position can only be redeemed from absurdity by showing proof that characterless existence is a legitimate postulate of thought—a proof which from the very nature of the case is impossible. And I know of no better way of putting the matter than by saying with Bradley,[91] "if it (the unknowable) actually were not knowable, we could not know that such a thing even existed. It would be much as if we said, "Since all my faculties are totally confined to my garden, I cannot tell if the roses next door are in flower." On such a theory as this we have vindicated the possibility of knowledge only to find that it involves us in a larger skepticism; for the intelligible world, whose existence has been validated against the doubt of Hume, turns out to be a subjective cosmos valid only within limits, which the intelligence that sees the limits is incapable in any way of understanding or explaining; while beyond those limits lies a world whose nature refuses to submit itself to thought. Each of these two worlds, according to Kant, determines the same manifold of sensation. The "determination of a sensible occurrence which can be the object of possible experience or inferred as an explanation of experience . . . . . its simple position of antecedence or sequence in time to other occurrences, as well as its relation to conditions which regulate that position and determine its sensible nature . . . . . will belong to one world of which a unifying self-consciousness is the organizing principle: while the very same occurrence, as an effect of things-in-themselves, will belong to another world, will be subject to a wholly different order of determinations, which may have —and indeed, in being so described, is assumed to have— some principle of unity of its own, but of which, because it is a world of things-in-themselves, the principle must be

[91] App. and Reality, p. 129—(parenthesis mine.)

taken to be the pure negation of that which determines the world of experience."[92]   If this be so, man's conception of his universe is, as Green points out, an unwarrantable one.   Man has, indeed, built up a universe out of the principles of his own thought but as these principles are only his private and subjective possession and of no universal applicability, and inasmuch as we have warrant for asserting the *existence* of a world to which they cannot be applied, there seems to be no reason for putting a limit to any number of such private universes.   " We have," thus, "asserted the unity of the world of our experience only to transfer that world to a larger chaos."   But the truth is that there is no such world, for the very idea of a world unrelated to thought is a contradiction.   It is no doubt true that the world is more than *my* thought as the thought of a finite individual compelled by the very limitation of my finitude to know the world only in a piecemeal and fragmentary way ; but it is not true that it can exist unrelated to *any* thought.[93]   There is no doubt "a world real and independent of the individual's transient acts of knowledge," but this gives no justification for asserting that there is a world "divorced from intelligence altogether."   It has already been shown that thought can never pass beyond experience,[94] however necessary it may be to pass beyond direct experience to an experience indirect and still more widely organized.   'What lies beyond experience' either means further experience or means —*nothing.*   The individual as knower does not stand outside the real, subjugating it to his intellectual purposes by the use of categories which are essentially foreign to it ; on the contrary, "the knower is in the world which he comes to

[92] Prolegomena, etc., p. 42.

[93] " The fact that falls elsewhere seems, in my mind, to be a mere word and a failure, or else an attempt at self-contradiction.   It is a vicious abstraction whose existence is meaningless nonsense, and is therefore not possible."—Bradley's App. and Reality, p. 145.

[94] Cf. also Green's Works, Vol. I, p. 487.—" There is no possible inference from experience to what is beyond experience."

know, and the forms of his thought, so far from being an alien growth or an imported product, are themselves a function of the whole. As a French writer puts it, 'consciousness so far from being outside reality, is the immediate presence of reality to itself and the inward unrolling of its riches.' " [95] Nor will it do to try to evade the consequences of this position by claiming that it succeeds in concealing within itself two propositions, the meanings of which are really different, but which the philosopher by a process of idealistic legerdemain succeeds in presenting as one, the two propositions, "that a thing is only conceivable by thought" and "that the thing only exists for thought." While the meanings of the two are indeed different, they are yet both justifiable; the former, however, is the comparatively trivial assertion that inasmuch as thought is "the faculty that conceives," the conception of a thing can only be mediated by thought—a proposition barren enough to be accepted by all parties, independently of their deeper philosophical views. It is the latter which is of real interest and which constitutes the essence of that idealistic interpretation of the world for which the present writer contends. It is the latter too, against which a mistaken dualism [96] contends, under the thoroughly erroneous impression that it jeopardizes the existence of an objective or external world. The truth is, rather, that the idea of an objective world finds ultimate justification for itself in terms which the idealistic logic alone can supply. Such idealism as Green's finds the existence of an external world as stubborn and as unalterable a fact as it is believed to be by any dualist that lives. The real difference between idealism (of the objective type) and dualism is fundamentally misinterpreted when it is made to rest upon the existence of an external world; for their real difference turns upon the analysis of what externality or ob-

---

[95] Seth's Two Lectures on Theism, p. 19.

[96] I am speaking of metaphysical dualism ; not of the dualistic assumptions of an empirical science like psychology—assumptions which are as justifiable as they are provisional.

jectivity implies. As Green maintains, "it is not the conception of fact, but the conception of the consciousness for which facts exist, that is affected by such analysis (that is, the idealist's analysis)."[97] While, then, both the above propositions are true, it must, nevertheless, be acknowledged that it is not possible to pass from the former to the latter without further justification, and it must also be acknowledged that the opponent of idealism is justified in accusing of subjectivity any theory which uses the former as the logical ground for claiming the latter. We cannot assert, without more ado, that thought is the condition of the existence of reality "because all reality requires thought to conceive it." "But it is another matter," as Green claims, "if, when we come to examine the constituents of that which we account real — the determinations of things — we find that they all imply some synthetic action which we only know as exercised by our own spirit. Is it not true of all of them that they have their being in relations; and what other medium do we know of but a thinking consciousness in and through which the separate can be united in that way which constitutes relation ? We believe that these questions cannot be worked out without leading to the conclusion that the real world is essentially a spiritual world, which forms one interrelated whole because related throughout to a single subject. And the same process will help us to understand our own inveterate supposition to the contrary. It will show us that this is due to an abstraction and confusion incidental to a certain stage of our intelligence; an abstraction by which we detach certain relations from the totality of the world, a confusion by which, having designated these relations as 'matter' we assume an independent entity corresponding to that name and opposed to that spiritual activity on which the relations that constitute matter, like all others, really depend for their existence."[98] This is a con-

---

[97] Prolegomena, etc., p. 69. The words in parenthesis are mine.

[98] Green's Work, Vol. III, p. 144.

clusion which Kant's thinking leads up to but fails to draw. Having shown, with a logic which is incapable of being refuted, that self-consciousness is a principle necessary for the constitution of an objective world of order and fact, he yet warns us against inferring anything as to the "spirituality of the real world." The world which the understanding has made is a world merely of phenomena, and the conclusions drawn concerning this world are limited to it and have no legitimate application to the 'real' world which is the world of things-in-themselves. And in connection with this claim, a further distinction is made between what he calls the form and the matter of the phenomenal world (nature). "*Natura formaliter spectata* is the work of the understanding; but *natura materialiter spectata* is the work of unknown things-in-themselves, acting in unknown ways upon us."[99] The result, however, of such a position would really be a skepticism more profound than that from which Kant was trying to rescue Philosophy; and the cure for this skepticism is only to be had by recognizing that when we have "excluded from things-in-themselves every kind of qualification arising from determination by or relation to an intelligent subject" all the meaning which was supposed to be contained "in the assertion of a dependence of this subject upon them" has been evaporated.[100] But when the unmeaning character of this unknowable world has been shown, we are compelled to give up forever any existence unrelated to thought, and the next step which follows logically is the assertion of an universal thinker whose existence, so far from being the hypostasis of an abstraction, is the only genuine and absolute reality of which we can form any con-

---

[99] Prolegomena, etc., p. 41.

[100] The attention of those critics of Green, who object to his doctrine of the unreality of 'mere feeling,' may be called to another doctrine of his (which these critics usually ignore) viz.—the unreality of 'mere thought.'—"We admit that mere thought can no more produce the facts of feeling, than mere feeling can generate thought. But we deny that there is such a thing as 'mere feeling' or 'mere thought,' etc."—Proleg., etc., p. 53.

ception.   " Objective nature must indeed be something else
than ourselves and our states of consciousness as we are apt
to understand these when we falsely abstract our states of
consciousness from their conditions and ourselves from relation to the world; but it does not follow that it is other than
our states of consciousness in their full reality, *i. e.*, in the
fullness of those relations which pre-suppose relation to
an eternal subject. I do not 'make nature' in the sense
that nature=a succession of states of consciousness, beginning with my birth and ending with my death. If so, the
'objectivity' of nature would doubtless disappear; there
would be as many 'natures' as men. But only by a false
abstraction do we talk of such a succession of states.
Their reality lies in eternal relations which are there
before what I call my 'birth,' and after my 'death,' if
'before' and 'after' had any proper application to them;
and only through these relations are they known; only
through them do they form an experience. That kind
of subjectivity which alone is incompatible with their being
objective, *i. e.*, determined by permanent and necessary
laws, lies merely in our misunderstanding of them. 'But
how,' it may be said, 'can I misunderstand them if I am the
eternal subject out of relation to which their reality, as an
order of nature, arises ?' The eternal subject is me as *ego*,
but *not* as an ego determining all phenomena. If it were
not me, my knowledge would be impossible; there would be
no nature for me. If it were me in its full reality, as the
subject determining all phenomena, my knowledge would be
all knowledge." [101]   All of which goes to prove that Reality
in its ultimate significance must be categorized as personal
and spiritual. Green's constructive exposition of this,
together with his subtile and discriminating defense of it,
constitutes one of the most valuable contributions to the
metaphysical thinking of Britain during the last twenty-
five years.

[101] Green's Works, Vol. II, p. 32,—The 'Deduction of the Categories' in the
first edition of the Critique.

BIBLIOGRAPHY.

S. Alexander.	Moral Order and Progress.
C. Bakewell.	Philosophical Review, July, 1898. Pluralism and Monism.
J. M. Baldwin.	Social and Ethical Interpretations.
	The Origin of a Thing and Its Nature. Princeton Contributions to Psychology, Jan., '96.
	Reality and Time. Psychological Review, Sept., '95.
A. J. Balfour.	Foundations of Belief.
	A Defence of Philosophic Doubt.
	Green's Metaphysics of Knowledge. Mind, Vol. IX.
E. Belfort Bax.	The Problem of Reality.
B. Bosanquet.	Logic. 2 vols.
	The Psychology of the Moral Self.
	The Essentials of Logic.
B. P. Bowne.	Theory of Thought and Knowledge.
	Philosophy of Theism.
F. H. Bradley.	Appearance and Reality.
	Mind. April, 1894.
B. C. Burt.	A History of Modern Philosophy. Vol. II, pp. 306–319.
E. Caird.	The Critical Philosophy of Kant. 2 vols.
	Essays on Literature and Philosophy. Vol. 2.
	Hegel. (Blackwood's Classics).
	Professor Green's Last Work. Mind, Vol. VIII, p. 546, etc.
	Evolution of Religion. Vol. I.
	The Social Philosophy of Comte.
J. Caird.	Spinoza.
	Philosophy of Religion.
H. Calderwood.	Another View of Green's Last Work. Mind, Vol. X.
Wm. Caldwell.	Psychological Review, July, 1898. On Titchener's View of the Self.
J. E. Creighton.	Is the Transcendental Ego an Unmeaning Conception? Philosophical Review, March, '97.
C. F. D'Arcy.	A Short Study of Ethics.
J. Dewey.	Mind, January, 1890. Some Current Conceptions of the Term 'Self.'
	The Philosophy of T. H. Green. Andover Review, Vol. XI.
	Green's Theory of the Moral Motive. Philosophical Review, Nov., '92.
A. Eastwood.	Lotze's Antithesis of Thought and Things. Mind, July and October, 1892.

A. Eastwood.   On Thought Relations.   Mind, April, 1891.

Mr. Balfour's Refutation of Idealism.   Mind, April, 1894.

C. C. Everett.   Fichte's Science of Knowledge.

W. H. Fairbrother.   The Philosophy of T. H. Green.

Ferrier.   Institutes of Metaphysics.

Kuno Fischer.   A Critique of Kant.

A. C. Fraser.   Gifford Lectures.   (First and Second Series.)

G. S. Fullerton.   Psychological Review, January, 1897.   The Knower in Psychology.

The Works of T. H. Green.   3 vols.

T. H. Green.   Prolegomena to Ethics.

R. B. Haldane.   Hegel.   Contemporary Review, February, '95.

Hegel and His Recent Critics.   Mind, Vol. XIII.

H. Haldar.   Green and His Critics.   Philosophical Review, March, 1894.

Hegel.   Philosophy of Religion.   3 vols.

Logic (Wallace).

Philosophy of Mind (Wallace).

L. T. Hobhouse.   The Theory of Knowledge.

J. R. Illingworth.   Personality Human and Divine.

Divine Immanence.

W. James.   The Will to Believe.

Psychology.   2 vols.

Psychological Review, March, 1895.   The Knowing of Things Together.

H. Jones.   The Philosophy of Lotze.

Idealism and Epistemology.   Mind, July, 1893.

Kant.   Critique of Pure Reason.

Theory of Ethics.   (Abbott's Tr.).

Prolegomena to any Future Metaphysic.

G. T. Ladd.   Philosophy of Knowledge.

Philosophy of Mind.

S. S. Laurie.   The Metaphysics of T. H. Green.   Philosophical Review, March, 1897.

J. A. Leighton.   Hegel's Conception of God.   Philosophical Review, November, 1896.

Lotze.   Microcosmus.

Metaphysics.   2 vols.

Philosophy of Religion.

Outlines of Metaphysics.

Outlines of Psychology.

Practical Philosophy.

J. S. Mackenzie.   Mr. Bradley's View of the Self.   Mind, July, '94.

Dean Mansel.   Philosophy of the Conditioned.

Limits of Religious Thought.

E. B. McGilvary.   The Presupposition Question in Hegel's Logic.   Philosophical Review, Sept., '97.

The Dialectical Method.   Mind, Jan., April, July, '98.

J. L. McIntyre.   Mind, July, 1895. Time and the Succession of Events.
J. M. E. McTaggart.   Studies in Hegelian Dialectic.
J. S. Mill.   Examination of Sir W. Hamilton's Philosophy, Vol. I.
G. Morris.   Kant. (Grigg's Philosophical Classics.)
J. H. Muirhead.   The Goal of Knowledge. Mind, Oct., 1897.
A. T. Ormond.   Basal Concepts of Philosophy.
    The Negative in Logic. Princeton Contributions, etc., Sept., '97.
F. Paulsen.   Introduction to Philosophy.
A. Riehl.   An Introduction to the Theory of Science and Metaphysics.
D. G. Ritchie.   Darwin and Hegel.
    Mind. 1888, pp. 257, etc.
    The One and The Many. Mind, Oct., 1898.
    The Relation of Metaphysics to Epistemology. Philosophical Review, January, '94.
J. Royce.   The Conception of God.
    Philosophical Review, September, 1894. The External World and the Social Consciousness.
    Philosophical Review, September and November, 1895. Self-Consciousness, Social Consciousness and Nature.
    Spirit of Modern Philosophy.
    Religious Aspect of Philosophy.
    Studies in Good and Evil.
Saisset.   Modern Pantheism. 2 vols.
F. C. S. Schiller.   Riddles of the Sphinx.
    Mind, January, 1895. The Metaphysics of the Time-Process.
    Reality and Idealism. Philosophical Review, Sept., '92.
A. Seth.   Man's Place in the Cosmos.
    Two Lectures on Theism.
    Scottish Philosophy.
    Hegelianism and Personality.
Seth and Haldane.   (Edited by) Essays in Philosophical Criticism.
A. Seth.   Psychology, Epistemology and Metaphysics. Philosophical Review, March, '92.
    Epistemology in Locke and Kant. March, '93.
    Epistemology of Neo-Kantism. May, '93.
    From Kant to Hegel.
    Epistemology and Ontology. Philosophical Review, Sept., '94.
    The Problem of Epistemology. Philosophical Review, Sept., '92.
H. Sidgwick.   A Dialogue on Time and Common Sense. Mind, Oct., '94.
    Green's Ethics. Mind, Vol. IX, p. 169, etc.
J. M. Sterrett.   Studies in Hegel's Philosophy of Religion.
G. F. Stout.   The Genesis of the Cognition of Physical Reality. Mind, January, '90.
J. Tufts.   Philosophical Review, July, '98. Epistemology and Mental States.

J. Tufts.   Can Epistemology be Based on Mental States? Philosophical
                         Review, 1897.
C. B. Upton.   The Hibbert Lectures.   1893.
                       Theological Aspects of the Philosophy of T. H. Green.   The
                         New World, March, '92·
W. Wallace.   Prolegomena (To Hegel's Logic).
J. Watson.   Idealism and Christianity.
                       An Outline of Philosophy.
                       The Absolute and the Time-Process. Philosophical Review,
                         July and Sept., '95·
                       Schelling's Idealism (Grigg's Classics).
                       Kant and His English Critics.
                       The Problem of Hegel.   Philosophical Review, Sept., '94·
                       Metaphysic and Psychology.   Philosophical Review, Sept., '93·
L'idéalisme de Th. Hill Green, Revue de Métaphysique et de la Morale, Nov. 1896.